October Ogre

"Oh no, look!" Nate whispered. He scrunched back into the fake-fur blanket.

The figure was wearing torn, dirty clothes, as if he had just crawled out of a grave. The space over his shoulders, where his head should have been, was empty.

The zombie held out a basket. The kids looked inside. A dead-looking face stared back at them!

October Ogre

RING BELL FOR SERVICE

by Ron Roy

illustrated by
John Steven Gurney

A STEPPING STONE BOOK™

Random House 🏠 New York

This book is dedicated to Oliver.
—R.R.

To Molly
—J.S.G.

Visit us on the Web!
ronroy.com
randomhouse.com/kids

Educators and librarians, for a variety of teaching tools, visit us at
RHTeachersLibrarians.com

Library of Congress Cataloging-in-Publication Data
Roy, Ron.
October ogre / by Ron Roy ; illustrated by John Steven Gurney.
p. cm. — (Calendar mysteries) "A Stepping Stone Book."
Summary: Bradley, Brian, Nate, and Lucy visit a haunted hotel on Halloween, but once inside they realize that they have seen plenty of people going in and none coming back out.
ISBN 978-0-375-86888-7 (trade) — ISBN 978-0-375-96888-4 (lib. bdg.) —
ISBN 978-0-375-89971-3 (ebook)
[1. Mystery and detective stories. 2. Haunted houses—Fiction. 3. Halloween—Fiction. 4. Twins—Fiction. 5. Brothers and sisters—Fiction. 6. Cousins—Fiction.] I. Gurney, John Steven, ill. II. Title.
PZ7.R8139Oct 2013 [E]—dc23 2012038159

Printed in the United States of America

10 9 8 7 6 5 4 3

Contents

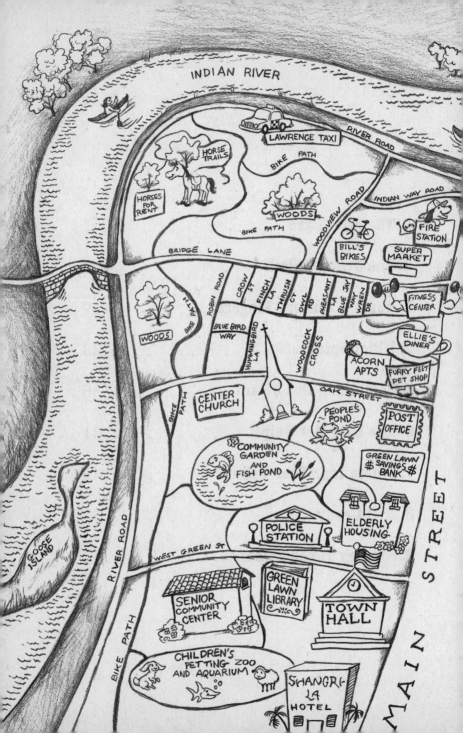

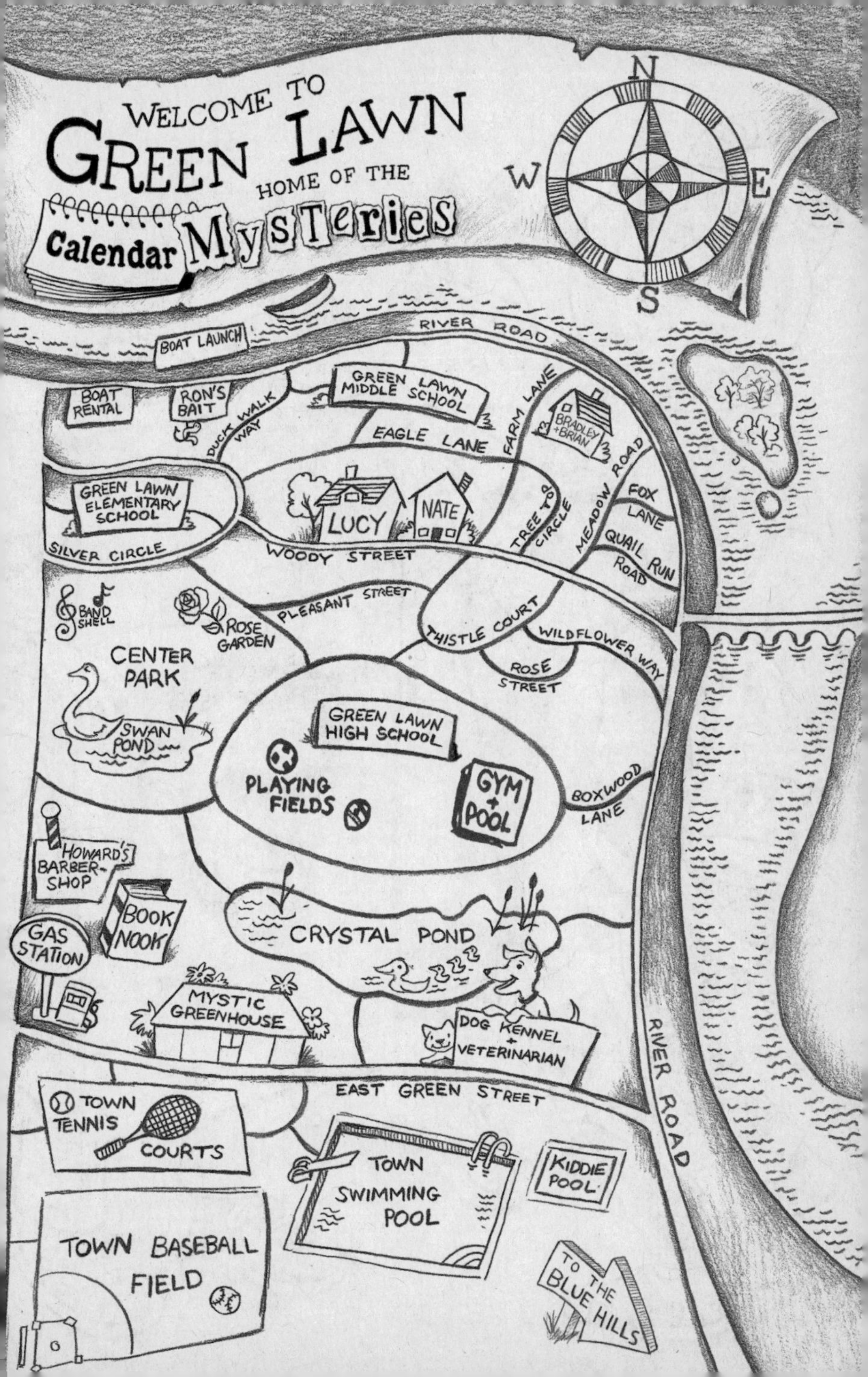
WELCOME TO
GREEN LAWN
HOME OF THE
Calendar Mysteries
N
W
E
S
BOAT LAUNCH
RIVER ROAD
BOAT RENTAL
RON'S BAIT
DUCK WALK WAY
GREEN LAWN MIDDLE SCHOOL
FARM LANE
BRADLEY + BRIAN
EAGLE LANE
MEADOW ROAD
GREEN LAWN ELEMENTARY SCHOOL
LUCY
NATE
TREE TOP CIRCLE
FOX LANE
QUAIL RUN ROAD
SILVER CIRCLE
WOODY STREET
PLEASANT STREET
BAND SHELL
ROSE GARDEN
THISTLE COURT
WILDFLOWER WAY
ROSE STREET
CENTER PARK
GREEN LAWN HIGH SCHOOL
SWAN POND
PLAYING FIELDS
GYM + POOL
BOXWOOD LANE
HOWARD'S BARBER-SHOP
BOOK NOOK
GAS STATION
CRYSTAL POND
MYSTIC GREENHOUSE
DOG KENNEL + VETERINARIAN
RIVER ROAD
EAST GREEN STREET
TOWN TENNIS COURTS
TOWN SWIMMING POOL
KIDDIE POOL
TOWN BASEBALL FIELD
TO THE BLUE HILLS

1
The First Ogre

"How do I look?" Bradley asked. He was wearing a cardboard box. His head stuck out through a hole in the top, and his feet came out the bottom. There were holes in the sides for his arms.

Bradley had pasted pictures of Presidents George Washington, Abraham Lincoln, Theodore Roosevelt, and Thomas Jefferson on the four sides.

"You look like a box of cereal," Nate said.

"What are you supposed to be?" asked Lucy.

Bradley grinned. "I'm Mount Rushmore," he said.

It was Halloween, and the kids were getting dressed at Nate's house. They were going to the Shangri-la Hotel. For Halloween, the building had been changed into a haunted house. All the kids they knew were planning to be there.

Bradley's twin brother, Brian, was dressed as an astronaut. A clear plastic salad bowl covered his red hair. He pretended to breathe through a vacuum-cleaner hose taped to the bowl. His shirt and pants were covered with tinfoil.

Lucy was dressed as Sacagawea. She wore a fake-leather dress and moccasins and had her hair in a braid.

Nate had wound strips of rags around his face and body. "Guess what I am!" he said.

"Raggedy Andy?" Brian joked.

"No, I'm a mummy," Nate said.

The four kids were best friends. Bradley and Brian's older brother, Josh, was pals with Dink Duncan, Lucy's cousin. Nate's older sister, Ruth Rose, hung out with Josh and Dink.

The kids left Nate's house and walked to Main Street. The sun was down, but it was not quite dark. They waited at the traffic light in front of Howard's Barbershop.

"Dink told me there's an ogre's cave inside the hotel," Lucy said. "The ogre is guarding a basket of candy. If we steal candy without getting caught, we get a prize!"

"Cool," Brian said. "We get candy *and* a prize!"

When the sign said WALK, they crossed Main Street and headed to the Shangri-la Hotel. They stood behind some bushes and looked at the hotel.

"It *does* look haunted," Lucy said. Bats, witch faces, and skeletons peered out the windows. Thick cobwebs hung from the front door. Spooky music came through hidden speakers.

A tall green ogre stood at the door. The monster had a lumpy green face and a fat belly. He held a club in his chubby fingers.

"What an awesome ogre!" Brian said. "Let's go say hi!"

"Maybe not," Nate said. "I don't hang out with ogres."

A bunch of kids in costumes were gathering at the hotel entrance. Bradley saw a Miss Piggy, a Batman, and some ghosts wearing bedsheets. The ogre opened the door and let a few of the kids inside. One of them was wearing a red cowboy hat.

"Hey, that's Luke Sanders from our class!" Nate said, pointing. Nate waved,

but Luke had disappeared into the haunted house.

"Come on," Brian said. "Let's go in. Josh told us some of the high school kids helped decorate. He said it's real scary!"

Just then the hotel door creaked open. More kids went inside. The ogre stayed outside. He waved at Bradley, Brian, Nate, and Lucy.

"He's telling us to come over," Bradley said.

"Um, I'm not sure," Nate said. "I mean, I don't mind being scared, but that ogre guy is too creepy. Maybe I'll just hang out here."

Lucy took Nate's hand. "Come on, Nate. It'll be fun," she said. "And friends stick together! If you don't go in, we won't go in, either."

"But I want to go in!" Brian said. "I want to steal the candy and get a prize!" He looked at his brother. "What do you say, Bradley?"

"I love Halloween, too," Bradley said. "But I agree with Lucy. If Nate doesn't want to go in, we don't go in."

"Maybe later," Nate said. "I just need to think about it."

The kids sat near the bushes and kept their eyes on the haunted hotel. The ogre kept his eyes on *them*.

2
The Crabby Witch

Soon all the kids had gone inside the haunted hotel. Only Bradley, Brian, Nate, and Lucy were still outside.

"I wonder what they're doing in there," Lucy said.

"Getting eaten up by the ogre," Nate muttered.

"The ogre is still outside," Brian said. "I say we go in right now. I need candy!"

"How about you, Nate?" Lucy asked.

Nate looked at the ogre standing in front of the hotel. "Do you think it's really, *really* scary in there?" he asked.

"I hope so!" Brian said.

"Probably just average scary," Bradley said. "The adults who planned this wouldn't want to scare us to death!"

"Come on, Nate," Brian said. "We're the last ones out here. Those other kids are going to steal the candy and get the prize!"

Nate took a deep breath. "Okay, let's do it!" he said.

"Awesome!" Brian said, slapping Nate on the back.

Nate stood as tall as he could. "Who's afraid of some ogre?" he said.

"Not us!" they all yelled. Then they marched toward the hotel entrance. They stopped about ten feet from the ogre.

"Can I change my mind again?" Nate whispered.

"No!" Brian said.

"It does look real," Bradley whispered. Then he laughed. "But ogres *aren't* real!"

"It's just a costume," Lucy said.

The kids walked over to the ogre.

"Welcome to the haunted house," the ogre said. Bradley thought he'd heard that deep voice before.

"Follow me!" The ogre reached for the door. Bradley, Brian, Nate, and Lucy followed.

The door groaned when the ogre pulled it open.

The ogre tapped Bradley on the head. "Are you supposed to be a box of laundry soap?" he asked.

"N-no," Bradley stuttered. "I'm Mount Rushmore."

"Cool," the deep voice said. "Be careful inside."

Again, Bradley thought he recognized the voice.

"Be careful of what?" Nate asked.

The ogre laughed. "Everything!"

He stepped aside. Bradley and his cardboard box waddled through the door. Brian was right behind him, pushing his way in. Lucy was next, and Nate came last. He took very small steps.

The first thing Bradley noticed was the fog. It was like walking into a cloud. Foggy mist was all around them. Bradley could barely see his feet.

"Follow the green footprints," the ogre said.

Then the door creaked shut, and the kids were alone.

"What green footprints?" Bradley whispered.

The four kids were standing in the dark. Tiny lights on the ceiling blinked on and off through the mist.

"It's so *quiet* in here!" Bradley whispered. He wondered where all the other kids were.

Suddenly a tall witch appeared out of the mist. She shone a light into Bradley's eyes.

Bradley gulped. "Where did you come from?" he asked.

"From a daaaaarrrrk plaaaace," the witch hissed.

Brian and Lucy giggled. Nate moaned.

The witch wore a long black dress and a pointy hat. Bradley was sure he saw spiders crawling in her tangled hair. She had a crooked nose, a hairy wart, and gross teeth.

"You're late!" the witch said. She reached a skinny hand toward Bradley. Her fingernails were long and black. "Give me your hand!"

"No way!" Bradley said.

"Chill out," the witch said. "I just want to take you to the green footprints. Follow me."

The four kids followed the witch into the gloomy place.

"Um, Miss Witch?" Bradley said. "What happened to the other kids who came in here?"

"No questions!" she said, pointing to the floor. "Just follow these footprints!" Then the witch walked away.

"Why is she so crabby?" Nate asked.

Bradley saw big green footprints on the floor, glowing in the dark.

They were in the Shangri-la Hotel lobby. Bradley had been here lots of times. He remembered all the nice furniture, the soft carpet, the potted palm trees. The manager, Mr. Linkletter, was funny and nice to kids.

But now it was all different. The lobby had been turned into a big, dark cave. Most of the furniture was gone. A few couches and chairs were covered with white sheets. There was no Mr. Linkletter standing behind the counter. Foggy mist floated in the air. The room was as silent as a cemetery.

"I wonder where Luke and those other kids are," Bradley said. "We're the only ones in here."

"The witch said to follow the footprints," Brian said. "So let's go!" He put a foot on one of the glowing prints.

Lucy hurried after Brian. Bradley and Nate followed her. The fog swirled around them.

RING BELL FOR SERVICE

Bradley wished he had chosen a different costume. It was hard to walk inside a cardboard box. He also wished it weren't so dark. If the footprints hadn't been glowing, he wouldn't have been able to see them.

The prints led the kids past the lobby counter. But there was no phone, no computer, and no big clock on the wall.

Instead there were spiderwebs hanging from the ceiling. There were big black spiders dangling from the webs. A mean-faced jack-o'-lantern sat where the phone used to be.

A skeleton lay on the desk. Its mouth was open as if it were laughing!

Brian stopped dead. Lucy bumped into him.

"Oh no," Nate whispered. "The ogre ate some kid and left a skeleton!"

"Totally fake," Brian muttered.

"Look, it's made of plastic." Brian thumped the skeleton's arm.

Suddenly the skeleton sat up. It turned and faced the kids, shaking its bones.

The four kids screamed and raced away.

3
Yummy Mummy Fingers

They ran through the dark fog. Brian was laughing like crazy. Bradley bumped into something and fell. He landed on a couch. The other three kids piled on top of him. Bradley's hand touched something furry, and he yelled, "It's a wolf!"

They were all tangled up in each other's arms and legs. Bradley felt his Mount Rushmore box crunch.

Lucy started to laugh. "No, it's a fake-fur blanket!" she said.

Nate gasped. "Is *that* fake, too?" he

asked, pointing ahead of them.

Out of the mist, a white ghost floated toward them. It was wearing a sheet with holes cut out for the eyes. The ghost was carrying a plate.

"Have a yummy finger?" the ghost asked the kids.

The plate held what looked like bloody human fingers!

"I'm not eating any mummy's fingers!" Nate yelled.

"He said *yummy,* not *mummy,*" Brian said. "Besides, they're cookies!" He grabbed one and popped it in his mouth. "With raspberry frosting!"

Bradley and Lucy each took one.

"No thank you," Nate said politely.

"Excuse me," Bradley said to the ghost. "Have you seen a bunch of other kids? They came in a while ago."

The ghost laughed. "Follow the foot-prints," he said, then disappeared into the darkness.

The kids looked around. They saw more spiderwebs, and bats hanging from the ceiling.

"That ghost didn't answer my question," Bradley said.

"They never answer questions," Nate muttered.

Lucy giggled. "Ghosts are so *rude!*" she said.

Just then another figure appeared in front of them.

"Oh no, look!" Nate whispered. He scrunched back into the fake-fur blanket.

The figure was wearing torn, dirty clothes, as if he had just crawled out of a grave. The space over his shoulders, where his head should have been, was empty.

The zombie held out a basket. The kids looked inside. A dead-looking face stared back at them!

Nate yelled and tried to hide behind Brian and Lucy.

Bradley gulped. The head was just a scary face painted on a volleyball. "Sir, have you seen some other kids?" he asked the zombie. "They came in before us."

"Follow the green footprints," the zombie said. The voice came from inside his chest. Then he wandered away, carrying the head.

"How can he see where he's going?" Brian whispered.

"They keep telling us to follow these dumb footprints!" Bradley said. "Why wouldn't he tell me where those other kids are?"

"Because they ate them!" Nate wailed.

"Nate, ghosts and witches and ogres aren't real," Bradley said. "These are all fake guys."

"But what if zombies and ogres *were* real?" Nate insisted. "What if they really wanted to eat kids? They'd come to a fake haunted house like this one, and find lots of kids. Like us!"

Suddenly they heard a loud squealing noise.

"It sounds like a pig," Lucy said.

"Oh no!" Nate said. "One of the kids was dressed as Miss Piggy. The ogre got her!"

"What ogre?" Brian said. "The only ogre we saw was the one outside. And that was just some grown-up in a costume."

"Can we leave now?" Nate asked. "I've had enough Halloween forever!"

"We can't leave," Bradley said. "We have a mystery to solve!"

"What mystery?" Nate asked.

"Nate, a bunch of kids came in here before us," Bradley said. "Now they're all gone! What if something happened to them?"

"Let's go find them!" Brian said. "It'll be like playing hide-and-seek in the dark!"

"I'm not going anywhere!" Nate said. He pulled the fake-fur blanket up to his chin. "I'll just stay here on this nice couch."

Brian tickled him. "What if that zombie comes back to get *your* head?" he asked.

"Come on, Nate," Lucy said. "The

ogre, the witch, the ghost, and that headless guy all told us to follow the footprints, right? So they must have told the other kids the same thing. Maybe the footprints will lead us to Luke and the others."

"We should split up and look around this place," Brian said.

"No way!" Nate said. "I'm not poking around a creepy hotel alone!"

"You won't be alone," Bradley said. "I'll be with you. Brian and Lucy will be the other team. If anyone finds those kids, yell out, okay?"

"We'll meet back here in fifteen minutes," Brian said.

"If we don't get eaten," Nate muttered.

"First, I'm getting rid of this," Bradley said. He wiggled out of the cardboard box and dropped it behind the couch.

"Okay, let's split up," Brian said.

"Come on, Lucy. Let's follow these foot-prints."

The pair disappeared in the fog.

"Now it's just us," Nate whispered to Bradley.

4
Killer Spiders!

Since Brian and Lucy had followed the footprints, Bradley and Nate walked in the opposite direction.

The foggy mist made it hard to see the dark floor. They stumbled into covered furniture and fake trees. Thick, sticky cobwebs hung from the branches.

Nate almost bumped into a long snake hanging from a tree branch. "It's a python!" Nate cried. "They can swallow a kid whole!"

"Nate, it's a fake snake," Bradley said. He patted the snake's rubber belly. "This guy can't swallow anything!"

"There should be a law against scaring little kids," Nate grumbled.

Bradley continued walking, feeling his way in the dark, misty place. Nate walked right behind him, holding on to Bradley's shirt.

They came to another fake tree. A sign on it said PULL THE WITCH'S BROOM HANDLE.

Bradley looked up. One branch was a broom. The handle had been painted white, and it glowed in the dark.

"Should we pull it?" he asked Nate.

"No way!" Nate said. "If you do, I'll bet we fall right into that witch's oven!"

Bradley laughed. He reached up and tugged on the broom handle.

They heard a creak. Then hundreds of tiny spiders dropped into their hair and faces.

"KILLER SPIDERS!" Nate screamed. "RUN!"

Bradley spit out a spider that had landed in his mouth. "They're plastic, Nate," he said. "Tiny plastic spiders."

"Boy, do I hate Halloween!" Nate said. He shook a bunch of the spiders out of his hair.

"Shhhh," Bradley said. He clamped a hand over Nate's mouth. "Do you hear something?"

It was like a voice coming from underwater. It sounded hollow and scary.

"People are yelling!" Nate said.

"Maybe it's Luke and those other kids," Bradley said.

"Or it could be your brother and Lucy," Nate said. "Maybe the witch is cooking them!"

"Can you tell where the sounds are coming from?" Bradley asked.

They both peered into the gloomy room. All they saw was mist, darkness, and the twinkly ceiling lights.

"Look, there's an exit sign!" Nate said. He took Bradley's shoulders and turned him around.

Bradley saw the red exit sign high on one of the walls.

"We can get out of here!" Nate said. "I've got my allowance money. I'll buy us ice cream at Ellie's Diner!"

"We can't just leave, Nate," Bradley

said. "What about those missing kids? Besides, we're supposed to meet Brian and Lucy in a few minutes."

Suddenly they heard another yell. This time it was closer. Bradley recognized Lucy's voice yelling, "BRIAN!"

"It's Lucy!" Bradley said. "Maybe she and Brian found those other kids."

Bradley shouted back, "Lucy, where are you?"

"Over here!" came Lucy's voice. "Follow the green footprints!"

"Okay!" Bradley shouted. To Nate he said, "Help me find those footprints again."

"How do we know that's really Lucy?" Nate asked. "It could be the witch, pretending to be Lucy!"

"It's Lucy," Bradley said. He tugged Nate toward where he thought the voice had come from.

They kept walking through the

darkness. Soon Bradley could make out the glowing footprints. "Here they are," he said.

"Here who are?" Nate whispered.

"The footprints," Bradley said.

They followed the glowing green prints. But a minute later, the footprints stopped. So did Bradley. Nate bumped into him.

"What's wrong?" Nate asked.

Bradley felt Nate's breath on the back of his neck.

"No more footprints," Bradley said in a low voice. "They just ended."

Bradley looked up. Even the twinkling lights were gone. He and Nate were standing in total darkness. No tiny lights, no glowing footprints. Just the misty fog and blackness all around them.

"I don't like this," Nate murmured. "Whoever invented Halloween should go to jail!"

"It's like a cave," Bradley whispered.

He remembered one time when he and Brian were playing ghost in their grandmother's attic. Bradley had hidden behind an old mattress, and Brian shut off the light to scare him. The attic felt—and *smelled*—just like this!

"This is weird," Bradley said. He reached his arms straight out into the darkness.

His fingers touched something soft and smooth. It felt like velvet cloth.

Suddenly a black curtain parted. Bradley gulped.

A bright light revealed Lucy standing like a statue. Behind her was a giant ogre's mouth. The mouth was wide open, showing large white teeth.

5
Something Got Brian!

"Lucy, what's going on?" Bradley cried. "Where's Brian?"

"I don't know!" Lucy said. "He just disappeared! We were following the green footprints. When we got here, Brian saw the candy."

"What candy?" Nate asked. He looked around.

Lucy pointed into the ogre's mouth. A basket of candy sat between the ogre's upper and lower teeth. "Brian ran to take some candy. When he started to grab the

basket, the lights went out! When they came on again, the candy was still there, but Brian was gone."

"Maybe the ogre chewed him up and swallowed him!" Nate said. "Like a candy bar!"

"The ogre is made of cardboard," Lucy said. She knocked on one of the teeth.

Bradley walked behind the ogre face. The black curtain went all around the head. He found an opening in the curtain and peeked through.

"Guys, come here!" Bradley yelled.

Lucy and Nate ran behind the ogre head.

Bradley was standing next to an enormous black pot. Water was bubbling in the pot, and misty steam was flowing over the edges.

"I knew it!" Nate said. "That witch is making kid soup!"

Under the pot, there were red logs that looked as if they were burning. But the flames were fake, too.

Bradley peered into the pot, sweeping the fog away with his hand. "All I can see is water," he said.

"Look at this!" Lucy said. A sheet of paper had been taped to the pot. Lucy read from the paper:

HOW TO MAKE WITCHY STEW

BOIL TEN GALLONS OF WATER.

MIX IN TWO CUPS OF BAT BLOOD.

DROP IN THREE SMALL CHILDREN.

STIR IN CHOPPED ONIONS AND CARROTS.

ADD SALT AND PEPPER TO TASTE.

WHEN DONE, POUR INTO BOWLS.

SERVE WITH CRACKERS.

"Three small children!" Nate cried. "The witch cooked Luke and Miss Piggy and Brian!"

"She didn't cook anybody," Lucy said. "The water in the pot isn't boiling." She put her hand on the pot. "Just a little warm."

"Then why is the water bubbling and making steam?" Bradley asked.

"It's Halloween magic," Nate said. "When I become president, we'll skip over Halloween and go right to Thanksgiving!"

"Guys, I'm worried about Brian and those other kids," Bradley said.

He walked around to the back of the pot. Something soft squished under his foot.

"AHHH!" he yelled, thinking he'd stepped on a bat.

But when he looked down, he saw a red cowboy hat. He picked it up and showed the others. "Luke was wearing a hat like this," he whispered.

The three kids just stared at the red hat.

"Maybe it's a clue," Nate said. "Maybe some monster grabbed Luke, and Luke left his hat so we'd find it!"

Lucy and Bradley looked at Nate. "There *are* no monsters!" Lucy said.

"Luke's hat was near this ogre's head," Bradley said. "It's almost like he was trying to tell us something!"

"It means Luke got this far, then he disappeared," Lucy whispered. "Just like Brian did."

6
The Kids Get Help!

The three kids backed away from the giant cardboard ogre. It stared at them with red eyes. The basket of candy sat on the ogre's tongue.

"I don't want to disappear," Nate said.

"Wait a minute! I just remembered something," Bradley said. "Brian said we should all meet back at that couch. So maybe he's waiting for us."

"Let's go and look," Lucy said.

"Good idea!" Nate said. "Rubber

snakes and killer spiders are better than disgusting ogres!"

The kids slipped through the black curtain again. They followed the glowing footprints past the fake trees and cobwebs.

They found the couch with the fake-fur blanket, just the way they'd left it. The tiny ceiling lights twinkled. The red exit sign glowed through the mist.

"No Brian," Lucy said.

"I'm getting scared," Bradley said. "Where could he be?"

"I'll bet he's with Luke and those other kids," Nate said. "Inside the ogre's fat tummy!"

"What do you think we should do, Lucy?" Bradley asked.

"Keep looking, I guess," Lucy said.

"How about you, Nate?" Bradley asked. "Want to keep looking?"

"No," Nate said. "I think we should

go to the police station. We need to tell Officer Fallon what's going on!"

"But we don't *know* what's going on," Lucy said.

"A bunch of kids disappeared. That's what's going on!" Nate insisted.

Bradley sat and thought about Brian disappearing. He thought about Luke's red hat on the floor.

Then he had another thought: *Maybe Nate is right! Maybe that big green ogre out front wasn't someone in a costume!*

Bradley left the cowboy hat on the couch. "I don't know if Officer Fallon will still be in his office," he said. "I think it's pretty late. I wish we could find a clock!"

"Let's go look behind Mr. Linkletter's desk," Lucy suggested.

The three kids hurried across the dark room. After a few minutes, they saw the plastic skeleton again.

Then Bradley had an idea. "Maybe we can *call* Officer Fallon!" he said. "If we leave the hotel, we might not be able to get back in again."

"There's no phone," Nate said.

Lucy poked around behind the desk. She pulled open drawers and searched on bookshelves.

"Here it is!" she said, holding the phone over her head.

She called information and asked for the Green Lawn police station.

She looked at Bradley and Nate. "What should I tell him?" she asked.

"Tell him Brian is missing," Bradley said.

Bradley and Nate could hear the phone buzzing in Lucy's ear. Then she said, "Hello, is this Officer Fallon?"

Lucy began to explain how Brian and the other kids had disappeared inside the haunted house. After a minute, she hung up.

"He's coming right over," she told the others.

Bradley looked around. He spotted the exit sign over the door. "Let's wait there," he said.

Three minutes later, they heard banging on the door.

"Who is it?" Nate asked.

Bradley giggled. "A ghost," he whispered in Nate's ear.

"Officer Fallon!" a deep voice shouted from outside. "Open up!"

Bradley pulled open the door, making a loud creak. Officer Fallon stepped inside. He looked brave and determined.

"Mr. Linkletter should oil this door," Officer Fallon said.

"He isn't here, either!" Bradley said.

"Hmph," Officer Fallon said. "Mr. Linkletter's gone, too? Very mysterious!"

"We saw a witch and a ghost and a zombie," Nate whispered.

"Did you?" Officer Fallon said. "I hate zombies!"

"And they talked to us!" Lucy said.

"What did they say?" Officer Fallon asked.

"We tried to ask them where the other kids were," Bradley said. "But they just kept telling us to follow the green footprints."

"So we did!" Lucy said.

The foggy mist floated in the air. The lights on the ceiling glimmered.

"Can you show me exactly where you were when Brian disappeared?" Officer Fallon asked.

"Easy," Nate said. "We followed these footprints. Come on, I'll show you!"

The kids led Officer Fallon through

the darkness. They kept their feet on the green footprints.

Suddenly they all heard a scream.

Officer Fallon froze in his tracks. "What was *that*?" he asked.

7

Where Is Officer Fallon?

"That's one of the weird noises!" Nate said.

"Gives me goose bumps," Officer Fallon said.

They moved slowly forward.

"Watch out for the snake!" Lucy said when they came to the snake tree. "But it's only a rubber one."

Officer Fallon tickled the snake's belly as he walked past it.

"Where's this zombie you told me about?" he whispered.

"I don't know," Bradley said.

"We don't know where the witch and ghost are, either," Lucy said.

"Everyone is disappearing," Nate muttered.

The green footprints led them to the couch. The fake-fur blanket was still there, but it was neatly folded. The cowboy hat sat on top of the blanket.

"This looks different," Bradley said. "Who folded the blanket?"

"Not me!" Nate said. "I never fold anything. Just ask my mother."

"I didn't do it, either," Lucy said.

"Is this Luke's hat?" Officer Fallon asked.

"Yes," Nate said.

Officer Fallon hitched up his pants. "Take me to this ogre head!"

They crept through the foggy mist to the black curtain. Lucy opened it at the crack.

"There it is!" Nate said. He pointed at the giant ogre's head.

"Oh my gosh!" Officer Fallon said. "It sure is big!"

"Come and see this!" Nate said. He took Officer Fallon's hand and led him to the other opening in the curtain. He showed him the cauldron of bubbling water. "It's a witch stew!"

Officer Fallon went right to the recipe. *"Three small children!"* he said. "Goodness, do you think the witch wants to cook some kids?"

"Yes!" Nate said.

"No," Lucy said. She put her hand on the pot. "The water isn't even hot."

Officer Fallon peeked into the pot. "It's dry ice," he said.

"What's that?" Bradley asked.

"Dry ice is made from carbon dioxide instead of water," Officer Fallon said. "When you drop it in warm water, the water and carbon dioxide make steam. Like in this pot. The water bubbles, but it never gets hot."

They all heard a voice. It sounded as if it came from underwater. The voice was moaning.

Nate grabbed Bradley's arm. Lucy grabbed his other arm.

"Who is it?" Nate whispered.

Bradley gulped. He had heard that voice before. "I think it's Brian," he whispered.

"How can you tell?" Lucy asked. "It's just a moaning sound."

"I know Brian's voice," Bradley said. "It's the same as mine!"

Bradley made the same sound. "See, we sound just alike," he said. "Sometimes at night Brian and I hide under our beds and make creepy noises to scare Josh."

"Yeah, I tried doing that once to scare Ruth Rose," Nate said. "But she's not scared of anything!"

They heard the moan again.

"Did you hear that, Officer Fallon?" Nate asked.

But Officer Fallon was gone.

"Where is he?" Lucy asked. "He was right behind us."

"Well, he's not here now!" Bradley said.

They dashed back through the black curtain. The giant ogre head was still staring at them. The basket of candy was still inside the ogre's mouth. But Officer Fallon was nowhere to be seen.

Bradley stepped on something that crinkled under his foot. He picked it up. "It's a candy wrapper," he said.

"Here's another one!" Nate said, grabbing a wrapper off the floor. "They're the same as the candies in the ogre's basket!"

Bradley stared at the basket of candy. "Officer Fallon loves candy," he said. "But he would never throw the wrappers on

the floor. He's always picking up litter!"

"Maybe he left the wrappers as clues," Lucy said.

"What good are clues?" asked Nate. "The ogre got him, like he got Brian and Luke and those other kids!"

8
Evil Candy

"I can't believe Officer Fallon just disappeared," Lucy said. "He was standing right here three seconds ago!"

"Maybe it's the candy," Nate said. "You eat some, and you disappear!"

"Dink told me that if we stole candy from the ogre, we'd get a prize," Lucy said.

"Some prize," Nate mumbled. "Eat it and you're gone."

They all stared at the basket in the ogre's mouth.

Bradley grinned at Nate. "Why don't you take a candy and find out what happens?"

"No way!" Nate said. "Why don't *you* take some, brave Bradley? Then Lucy and I will watch you disappear!"

Bradley shook his head. "No, I have to stick around to protect you from the witches and zombies."

"I'm not taking candy, either," Lucy said. "But I have an idea." She parted the black curtain. "I'll be right back."

Then she was gone.

"Where's she going?" Nate asked. "Now there are only two of us! If you disappear, I'll be all alone in this creepy place!"

"Don't worry," Bradley said. "I'm not going to disappear."

Nate peeked through the curtain crack. "It's dark out there," he said. "What if she—"

Suddenly Nate shrieked and jumped back. "Run for your life!" he yelled.

When Bradley turned, he saw a skeleton walking through the black curtain.

The skeleton pointed a bony finger at Nate. "Come with me, Nate Hathaway," the skeleton said. "I'm your new best friend!"

Nate ran and hid behind Bradley.

Bradley laughed. "Okay, come on out, Lucy," he said. "We know it's you."

Lucy stepped out from behind the skeleton and laid it on the floor. It grinned up at them through yellow plastic teeth.

"Where'd you get it?" Bradley asked.

"It was on Mr. Linkletter's desk, remember?" Lucy asked.

Nate walked over to Lucy and the skeleton. "Very funny," he said. "Why did you drag it way over here?"

"Mr. Skeleton is going to help us

figure out what happened to Brian, Officer Fallon, and the other kids," Lucy said.

"How's he going to do that?" Nate asked. "He doesn't have a brain, Lucy."

"No, but I do," Lucy said. She pulled a ball of string and some scissors from a pocket. "I borrowed these from Mr. Linkletter's desk."

"What're they for?" Nate asked.

"Maybe the skeleton can show us how everyone is disappearing," Lucy said. She cut a long piece of string from the ball. She tied one end of the string around the skeleton's left wrist. She tied the other end to his right wrist.

"Okay, pull on the string," Lucy said.

Bradley and Nate tugged on the string, and the skeleton's arms lifted off the floor.

"Perfect!" Lucy said. "Now help me stand it up."

Bradley and Lucy stood the skeleton on its feet.

"Move him over by the ogre," Lucy said.

They stood the skeleton in front of the ogre's mouth.

"Okay, I'll hold him up, and you two make him reach for the candy," Lucy said.

"How?" Nate asked. "I'm not getting near that candy!"

"Just pull the string up so his hands touch the basket," Lucy explained. "If I'm right, something should happen."

"Cool," Bradley said. "Like a skeleton puppet!"

Bradley and Nate lifted the string. The skeleton's bony hands moved forward. They touched the basket.

Nothing happened.

"Now make him take some candy," Lucy said.

Bradley and Nate pulled the string tighter. When the skeleton's hands landed on the candy, three things happened at once:

The lights went out.

They all heard a creaking noise.

Bradley and Nate yelled as the string was yanked from their fingers.

9
Bradley Takes a Chance

The lights came back on. The skeleton was gone.

"The cardboard ogre ate a plastic skeleton!" Nate said.

Lucy got down on her knees. She ran her fingers over the wooden floor where the skeleton had been standing. "Look, there are cracks here," she said.

Bradley dropped to his knees, too. "Yeah, and they're different from the regular cracks between the boards," he said. "They're wider."

Lucy looked closer. Her nose was almost on the floor. "These cracks are clean," she said. "There's no dust or dirt in them."

Bradley traced the cracks with his fingers. "They make a big square," he said, sitting up. "Guys, I think this is a trapdoor!"

Nate stepped back. "I'll bet they all fell into a dungeon or something!" he said. "Dungeons are filled with rats and spiders!"

Bradley pulled something from one of the cracks. "What's this?" he asked. What he held was thin, yellow, and curly.

Lucy took the object from Bradley's fingers. "It's a hair," she said. "My dolls have hair just like this."

Nate bent down for a look. "I think it's from Miss Piggy," he said.

All three kids stared at the floor.

"Miss Piggy is in the dungeon!" Nate cried. "This hair must have gotten caught when she fell through the trapdoor!"

Just then they heard a laugh. It came from under the floor.

"That's Brian!" Bradley said. "I'd know his laugh anywhere!"

"Why's he laughing?" Lucy asked.

"Maybe the rats are tickling him with their little feet!" Nate said.

Bradley looked down at his own feet. In his mind, he could see Brian reaching for that candy basket. He thought about Officer Fallon doing the same thing. He remembered the skeleton's fingers on the candy just before the lights went out.

Bradley jumped to his feet. He reached for the ogre's mouth. His hands shot past the cardboard teeth and he grabbed a handful of candy.

Suddenly the lights went out.

The trapdoor under their feet

creaked, then opened wide.

Bradley, Lucy, and Nate slid down a slippery chute. They landed on something soft.

Bradley could feel Nate's arms wrapped around him in the pitch-darkness.

"We're in the dungeon!" Nate yelled in Bradley's ear. "Now do you believe me?"

Bradley sat up. "Nate, we landed on a bed," he said. "Do dungeons have fluffy pillows and soft mattresses?"

"And I smell cookies and lemonade," Lucy added.

The lights came on. The plastic skeleton was hanging on the wall, grinning. About fifty kids were standing around the bed, pointing and laughing.

"You finally got here!" Luke Sanders said. "Did you find my hat?"

"Yeah, we found it," Bradley said.

"Why'd you leave it there?"

"It fell off when I came down the chute," Luke said.

"Hey, bro, what's up?" Brian said. He had taken off his salad bowl. He was grinning.

"What's going on, Brian?" Bradley asked. "We were really scared when we couldn't find you!"

"Sorry," Brian said. "I just tried to get

some candy, and I ended up down here!"

Someone in an ogre mask walked over to the bed. He pulled off the rubber mask. Underneath it was Officer Fallon's smiling face. "Welcome to the party!" he said. "All your friends are here."

Bradley looked around. He saw Miss Piggy. He saw the witch, the ghost, and the zombie. They had removed their costumes, too. The witch turned out to

be their teacher, Ms. Tery. The ghost was Ellie, who owned the diner. And the zombie was their friend Mr. Linkletter. They all waved at the kids.

"We wanted you kids to follow the green footprints," Officer Fallon said. "They led right to the ogre's head and the candy. When you touched the candy, a special trigger opened the trapdoor."

"So you knew the whole time?" Lucy asked.

"Yep. Everyone in town knew, except the kids," Officer Fallon said. "Were you surprised?"

"Totally!" Bradley said.

"This is awesome!" Lucy said.

"I wasn't surprised," Nate said, puffing up his chest. "I knew it was fake!"

Bradley bopped Nate with a pillow. "You did not! You were scared all along!"

Ellie walked over with a plate of cupcakes. They had orange frosting

and looked like small pumpkins. Nate grabbed one.

"Do you still hate Halloween?" Bradley asked his friend.

Nate's mouth was full. But he managed to say, "Nope!"

If you like Calendar Mysteries,
you might want to read
A to Z Mysteries!
Help Dink, Josh, and Ruth Rose . . .

. . . solve mysteries from A to Z!

Track down all these books for a little mystery in your life!

A to Z Mysteries®
by Ron Roy

Calendar Mysteries
by Ron Roy

Capital Mysteries
by Ron Roy

Ballpark Mysteries
by David A. Kelly

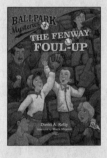

The Case of the Elevator Duck
by Polly Berrien Berends

Ghost Horse
by George Edward Stanley

How many of KC and Marshall's
adventures have you read?

Capital Mysteries